JACK
AND THE BEANSTALK

AN INTERACTIVE FAIRY TALE ADVENTURE

by Blake Hoena

illustrated by
Amit Tayal

raintree
a Capstone company — publishers for children

...t of Capstone Global Library Limited, a company incorporated
... having its registered office at 7 Pilgrim Street, London,
...red company number: 6695582

...co.uk

Text © Capstone Global Library Limited 2016
The moral rights of the proprietor have been asserted.

Edited by Kristen Mohn
Designed by Ted Williams
Creative Director: Nathan Gassman
Production by Tori Abraham

ISBN 978 1 4747 0717 6
19 18 17 16 15
10 9 8 7 6 5 4 3 2 1

British Library Cataloguing in Publication Data
A full catalogue record for this book is available from the British Library

Acknowledgements
Shutterstock: solarbird, background

Every effort has been made to contact copyright holders of material reproduced in
this book. Any omissions will be rectified in subsequent printings if notice is given to
the publisher.

All the Internet addresses (URLs) given in this book were valid at the time of going
to press. However, due to the dynamic nature of the Internet, some addresses may
have changed, or sites may have changed or ceased to exist since publication.
While the author and publisher regret any inconvenience this may cause readers,
no responsibility for any such changes can be accepted by either the author or
the publisher.

Printed in China.

CONTENTS

ABOUT
YOUR
ADVENTURE

Rip! You turn to see the ground tearing open and a huge vine sprouting out, reaching up for the sky. What on Earth? Of course there's only one thing to do – climb it and see where it takes you.

Chapter One sets the scene. Then you choose which path to take. Follow the directions at the bottom of the page as you read the stories. The decisions you make will change the outcome of your story. When you've finished one path, go back and read the others for new perspectives and more adventures.

Follow Jack's magical beanstalk and take this traditional tale to new heights ... if you don't fall to your doom!

A HANDFUL OF MAGIC

"What's taking so long?" Jack's mum yells.

Jack stares into the empty milking bucket and shakes his head. "Mum isn't going to like this," he mumbles, so that Milky White can't hear.

MOOOOO! she bellows as though she did hear.

"It'll be OK, Milky," Jack says, patting the cow's scrawny side. But he's not sure it will be. Milky hasn't produced a drop of milk in days.

Not wanting to face his mother, Jack drags his feet as he heads towards the house. When he gets there, his mother peers into the empty bucket. She lets out a heavy sigh.

7

"Selling milk was our only source of income," she cries. "How will we survive?" Jack's stomach grumbles in response. Neither of them have had much to eat lately, other than some watery soup.

"I suppose there is only one thing to do," Mum says. She looks at Milky White out in the pasture. *MOO!* the cow bellows again, knowing something unpleasant is about to happen. "If Milky White can't produce any more milk, we'll have to sell her."

Tears well up in Jack's eyes. "Do we have to?" he asks. "I'll take care of her."

"We can't afford to keep an old, dried-up cow," his mother replies sternly. "Take her to market. Trade her for something else we can use to earn money. Perhaps some chickens or a sheep."

With his head down, Jack walks over to Milky and ties a rope to her halter. "Let's go, old girl." Then they set out on the long, winding path into town.

He rounds a bend and hears a loud "Psssst!" A man standing at the side of the road, waves Jack over to him. "Good morning," the man says.

"Morning, sir," Jack replies.

"Where are you off to, lad?" the man asks.

"To market to sell our cow," Jack sniffs.

"You won't get much for a scrawny thing like her," the man says. "Shall we make a trade instead?"

"What sort of trade?" Jack asks.

The man reaches into his pocket. "Why, for a handful of these. You'll never be hungry again…"

9

IF THE MAN OFFERS JACK MAGIC BEANS, TURN TO PAGE 11.

IF THE MAN OFFERS JACK MAGIC NUTS AND BOLTS, TURN TO PAGE 44.

IF THE MAN OFFERS JACK MAGIC JACKS, TURN TO PAGE 77.

CHAPTER 2

A GIANT'S POINT OF VIEW

"Four thousand, seven hundred and twenty-nine," you count as you put a gold coin on top of the stack towering in front of you. You reach down into the sack at your feet, grab another and place it on top of the stack. "Four thousand, seven hundred and thirty..."

You are the giant Blunderbore, and this is your job: counting coins. It doesn't matter if they're gold coins, silver coins, brass coins, copper coins or chocolate coins. You spend hours each day happily counting them.

You're about to pick up the next coin when your wife, Fee Fie, lumbers into your counting chamber.

"Here you go, Blunniebuns," she says, putting down a cup. Time for tea!

As Fee Fie leaves, you glance out of the window. Outside your stone castle is a wide, rolling field dotted with trees. Beyond that, the tips of snowcapped mountains jut up from the land of Earth far below.

As you admire the scenery, you spot something peculiar. A large weed has appeared in the middle of your prized petunias.

TO CUT IT DOWN, GO TO PAGE 13.

TO LET IT GROW, TURN TO PAGE 26.

You can't have weeds crowding out your petunias! Next they'll be spreading to your peonies and pansies. You go outside, grab an axe, and stomp over to your garden. That's when you notice that the offensive plant isn't an ordinary weed.

It's a giant beanstalk.

And it has created a large chasm where it popped up through the ground. Peeking down into the hole, you see that the plant twists and twirls downwards until it disappears into the clouds.

What the…? You start chopping. *Thwack! Whack! Crack!*

The work is hard, and the beanstalk keeps sprouting up and sending out new shoots almost as fast as you can chop them. They snake around your ankles and tangle up your axe.

TURN THE PAGE.

As you're trying to free your axe from the stalk's vines, you think you can see a small creature scurry from beneath the leaves. Some little pest, you think. You get back to hacking. *Thwack!*

At last, around supper time, you seem to have the upper hand. The bothersome vine has stopped growing back and the petunias are no longer being pestered. You head towards the kitchen, your stomach rumbling.

"Fee Fie, oh hon, I smell some spuds and beef Wellington!" you shout. That's your favourite.

14

Fee Fie slams the lid down on a large black pot and spins around. "What? I know nothing about the blood of an Englishman!" she sputters as her eyes twitch nervously.

Your stomach grumbles again.

TO SEE WHAT'S IN THE POT, GO TO PAGE 15.

TO WAIT FOR FEE FIE TO BRING YOU SUPPER, TURN TO PAGE 27.

You're curious about the food, which smells unusual, so you lift the lid of the pot.

"No, don't!" Fee Fie shouts, but it's too late. You've already seen what she's hiding. Amongst the carrots and potatoes sits a boy.

"What's this?" you say to Fee Fie as she pretends to look surprised at seeing the boy in her pot. "What in the world?" You help the boy get out. "You know boys give me indigestion, Fee Fie."

TURN THE PAGE.

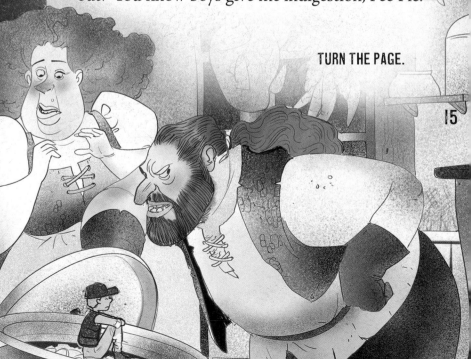

"You're such a fussy eater," Fee Fie complains.

You ignore her and lead the boy to your counting chamber. He tells you his name is Jack. "Here, let me give you something for your trouble," you say, handing him a small sack of gold coins.

"Wow! We can buy a new cow with this!" the boy exclaims, stew dripping from his clothes onto the floor. Then he looks at you cautiously. "So, you aren't going to eat me?"

"No, no," you say. "Boys aren't very tasty. Probably because they don't bathe very often."

Jack lets out a sigh of relief.

"Where did you come from?" you ask.

"I climbed up that beanstalk," Jack admits.

TO TAKE JACK BACK TO THE BEANSTALK, GO TO PAGE 17.

TO ASK JACK TO LEAVE, TURN TO PAGE 19.

As you walk Jack to the beanstalk, you see that it's grown back, bigger than before. It now towers above you. "I will give you an hour to get down," you warn. "Then I'm ripping this blasted thing up from its roots. It's done enough damage to my petunias!"

You also don't want anyone else climbing up and causing problems around here or, worse still, getting put into one of Fee Fie's stews. There are all sorts of strange creatures living down below, like boys made out of wood, and girls with incredibly long stringy hair. Yuck!

"Thank you, sir!" Jack says, shinnying down the stalk. "You're not so bad, for a giant!"

"And don't come back!" you yell, trying to sound threatening.

You sing to your petunias as you wait.

TURN THE PAGE.

The beanstalk continues to grow. It sends out new shoots that twist and tangle around everything near by. After an hour you wrap both arms around the beanstalk. You tug and yank and strain. Sweat pours down your giant brow.

"Heave!" With a loud rip the beanstalk's roots finally come loose. You let go and the beanstalk slips back through the chasm. Too late, you notice that some of its new shoots have wrapped themselves around your ankle. Before you know it, you're being dragged through the hole, too.

You claw and scratch at the soil, but it's no use. The weight of the beanstalk pulls you down. Down through the clouds to the little blue planet below.

"Awwwwww!" you scream. Who knows what miniature evils await you there…

18

THE END

TO FOLLOW ANOTHER PATH, TURN TO PAGE 9.

You show Jack to the door and tell him never to come back, if he knows what's good for him.

"I won't," he says. But his eyes twitch slightly, the way Fee Fie's do when she's up to something.

You go back to counting your coins. "Now where was I? Oh yes, four thousand, seven hundred and thirty-one…"

The next morning, before you begin counting your coins, you go out for a stroll. You walk over to the pond where your goose that lays golden eggs lives. You like to collect her eggs and then make them into coins, so that you have even more to count. But today she isn't there. You let that lad with the twitchy eyes go, and now your golden goose is missing! You put two and two together: Jack stole your goose.

TO GO LOOKING FOR JACK, TURN TO PAGE 20.

TO ASK YOUR WIFE ABOUT JACK, TURN TO PAGE 24.

You storm over to the beanstalk. You wedge

your large belly through the chasm and then start

shinnying down – down through the clouds, all

the way down to Earth. You finally land, panting

from the effort, and wonder briefly how you'll

get back up if coming *down* was that hard. You'll

worry about that later. You see a small cottage

that you decide must be Jack's.

Jack's mother steps out of the front door, having heard the great thud from your arrival.

"Have you seen my—" you start to say, enquiring about your missing goose. But Jack's mother interrupts.

"You! You must be that kind giant!" she gushes. "Thank you for that sack of gold. It was so nice of you not to eat my son."

"Well, boys are just too scrawny to eat," you admit. "Not like some other people I know." Jack's mother looks up at you, horrified. "Oh, no, no, I don't like the taste of mothers either," you say. "They're … um … too squishy."

21

Just then Jack comes strolling around the house holding your goose in his arms. "Look what I've got, Mum!" he says with a smile, which fades when he sees you.

TURN THE PAGE.

You are ready to pulverize him, but then you look around. Jack's house is a rundown shack. The fields look like they haven't grown a crop in years. And you could probably blow their barn over with one good sneeze. Jack and his mother don't have much. Perhaps you could forgive Jack's thievery just this once.

"Where did you get that goose, Jack?" his mother asks. "Should we cook it for dinner?"

"No, no! That's my special goose," you protest. You shudder at the thought of your golden goose being cooked. "Jack was ... looking after her for me."

"I was?" Jack asks, surprised.

You lean over and gently take the goose from Jack. With a wink, you say, "And Jack has agreed to work for me."

"I have?" Jack asks, still surprised.

"He has?" Jack's mother echoes.

Looking straight at Jack you growl, "Yes, in the garden. For wages. Or perhaps you'd rather help my wife ... in the kitchen?"

Jack gulps. "No! I like gardening!"

Jack's mother beams up at you. "How kind you are! It's so good of you to offer Jack a job."

You smother a laugh when you see the look on Jack's face. You pull him aside. "Every morning I want to see you trimming back that beanstalk of yours and pulling weeds from my garden," you say. "If not, I'll invite myself back ... for *dinner*."

23

You climb back up the beanstalk with your goose. From now on you can spend more time counting and less time weeding.

THE END

TO FOLLOW ANOTHER PATH, **TURN TO PAGE 9.**

"Fee Fie, oh hon!" you shout. "Have you seen that boy about?" You're angry. Angry enough to let her cook him in that pot.

Just then you hear a voice sing out, "Oh no, help! What shall we do? This young lad is stealing from you!" Your magic harp! At bedtime it sings you a lullaby. You can't fall asleep without it. You catch a glimpse of Jack sprinting past the kitchen door with the whimpering harp calling out again, "Help!"

You give chase. The boy runs for the beanstalk. He jumps onto it and with the harp wedged under his arm, he begins sliding down it.

The chasm in the ground isn't giant size, so it takes you a few minutes to squeeze through. Jack has already disappeared into the clouds, but still you follow. You are about halfway down when the beanstalk shudders.

Oh no! you think. Someone – Jack! – is chopping it down. And after all you did for that brat!

The stalk shudders again, then begins to sway. Suddenly it tips. You are falling, and there's nothing you can do. You land with an earth-shaking thud, leaving a giant-shaped hole in the pasture where Milky White once grazed.

25

THE END

TO FOLLOW ANOTHER PATH, **TURN TO PAGE 9.**

You wonder if the stalk might be a new exotic bean plant. You decide to let it grow and see what happens. For now you need to get back to counting. You don't stop until a loud rumbling comes from your tummy. Supper time! You get up, careful not to bump your desk and topple the stacks of coins. You head for the kitchen.

"Fee Fie, oh hon," you call out. "Do I smell stew and a sticky bun?"

"Ah!" Fee Fie exclaims, surprised to see you. She slams the lid down on a large black pot. "What? No! You do not smell the blood of an Englishman."

26

You give her an odd look. Fee Fie's hearing is not what it used to be. "Well, something definitely smells good," you say, sniffing the air.

TO ASK FEE FIE TO BRING YOU SUPPER, GO TO PAGE 27.

TO SEE WHAT'S IN THE POT, TURN TO PAGE 38.

You still have many more coins to count before bed, so you ask Fee Fie to bring your supper to your counting chamber when it's ready. Then you go back to counting.

"Seven thousand, two hundred and eight…" You are exhausted. As you count, you nod off.

You don't wake up until Fee Fie shouts, "Here you go, Blunderdear!" She puts your food down on the desk. Startled, you leap up from your chair. As you do, you bump your desk. Coins spill, tinkling and clinking all over the floor.

"Oh, sorry, Blunniekins," Fee Fie giggles as she scurries out the door.

You sigh. It takes you the rest of the night to recount your coins. And when you do finish, you discover that one sack of gold coins is missing.

TO GO AND LOOK FOR YOUR COINS, TURN TO PAGE 28.

TO ASK FEE FIE ABOUT THE MISSING COINS, TURN TO PAGE 30.

Where
could your
missing coins
be? You never
take them out of
your counting chamber.
You step outside to look.
That's when you see the beanstalk
rustling, and a boy with your sack of

coins crawling down it. "Hey, lad, come
back here!" you shout. He ignores you. You
run over to the beanstalk and shake it to get his
attention. What starts off as a small wiggle sends
growing vibrations through the stalk. Soon the
stalk is whipping back and forth.

The boy can't hold on. He is sent flying one way, and your gold the other. "Noooo!" you groan. You hate to lose even a single coin. It really messes up your counting.

Fee Fie appears. "What's wrong, Blunniebuns?"

"A boy stole a bag of my gold," you whine. "And they both fell somewhere down there."

"Noooo!" she cries. "I was marinating him for a new recipe!"

29

You shrug. At least you won't have to eat the scrawny boy for dinner.

THE END

TO FOLLOW ANOTHER PATH, **TURN TO PAGE 9.**

You storm off to the kitchen, calling, "Fee Fie, some of my coins are missing!"

"Oh my," she says, "I hope it wasn't that boy, Jack," she mumbles under her breath, but your giant ears hear it.

"What boy?" you ask.

"Oh, I confess! I had a boy in my pot," she explains. "He said he climbed up the beanstalk that sprouted between your petunias."

"And where is he now?" you ask, trying not to raise your voice.

"He was terribly dirty and turning my stew to mud," Fee Fie says. "I sent him to go and have a wash."

"Well I think he took some of my gold instead!" You rush outside to the garden. You crawl into the chasm that the beanstalk created.

You begin to climb down, but it's not easy. The beanstalk stretches down through a layer of clouds. It sways in the wind and sags under your giant weight. The rough stalk gives you painful splinters in your hands as you descend.

At the bottom you find a tiny little house that looks as though it's in need of some repairs. You knock on the small door with one giant knuckle, and a little woman peers out. Her eyes widen as she looks first at you, then at the beanstalk, then back at you. She looks ready to faint.

"Friend or foe?" she asks meekly.

"To be decided…" you say, trying not to growl.

"Well … why don't you come in before anyone sees you," she says. "People don't take kindly to giants around here."

TURN THE PAGE.

You crouch through the doorway, following her inside. You perch on a rickety chair, trying not to break it, and ask, "Who planted that beanstalk? Blasted thing sprouted up in my petunias."

"That was my son, Jack," the woman replies. "He traded our old cow for some silly magic beans, you see. I never thought they would grow."

With a quivering hand she puts a cup of "tea" in front of you, but it seems to just be hot water. Suddenly a boy bursts through the door. He proudly holds up your bag of coins. "Mum, look! Our problems are solved!" He skids to a stop when he sees you.

You look from the boy to his mother and then around the tiny room. It's a sorry sight.

TO GET ANGRY ABOUT THE STOLEN COINS, GO TO PAGE 33.

TO TAKE PITY ON JACK AND HIS MOTHER, TURN TO PAGE 36.

Poor or not, the boy shouldn't have stolen from you. "That's mine!" you shout, standing up. But you forget you are crouched inside a human house. Your head pokes up through the roof.

Shrieks and screams erupt from neighbours as they spot you. Soon men are rushing at you with pitchforks and axes.

Luckily for you, the house isn't much of a house. You simply shrug your shoulders and it crumbles around you. You run to the beanstalk, the villagers hot on your heels. You start to climb. The nimble villagers climb after you. After one painful poke in the bottom from one of their pitchforks, you have no choice but to boot them off the stalk. You send the man with the pitchfork flying with a mighty kick. Seeing this, the other villagers change their minds and quickly climb back down.

33

TURN THE PAGE.

You congratulate yourself on handling those pests. But you soon realize you are not out of danger. *Thwack!* The beanstalk shudders. *Whack!* Those little beasts are chopping down the stalk!

You climb faster. You reach up and grab the edge of the chasm just as the stalk collapses beneath you. For a moment you hang there. Then, with a grunt, you pull yourself up and go back inside your castle.

"Did you get your gold back?" Fee Fie asks.

"No," you growl as you storm past her.

"Well at least you got rid of that awful beanstalk," she says with a shrug.

No more beanstalk means no more mischievous boys. You suppose that's worth the cost of a small sack of gold.

THE END

TO FOLLOW ANOTHER PATH, TURN TO PAGE 9.

You are upset that Jack stole from you. But how can you be angry when they have so little?

"Jack, where did you get that?" Jack's mother shouts. "We aren't thieves!"

"It's OK," you say. "I have plenty of gold, and…" You don't want Jack to get into trouble with his mother. "And Jack earned it," you continue. "He did a few jobs for me – and my dear wife, Fee Fie. Isn't that right, Jack?" you say, giving Jack a stern look.

Jack gulps. "Um, yep. That's right!" Then he adds, "I worked really hard!" You give him a look that says *don't push it*.

You and Jack go outside. You ask him to cut down the beanstalk once you're safely home. "I might not be as generous with the next thief I catch," you warn.

Jack nods nervously.

You start your climb. Once you reach the top, the beanstalk shudders. Then it shakes. And suddenly it slips through the hole, into the clouds and disappears forever.

You happily go back to counting your coins, but you've lost your place. You have to start again. "One, two, three…"

THE END

TO FOLLOW ANOTHER PATH, TURN TO PAGE 9.

Thinking that Fee Fie is up to something, you lift the lid off the pot. You see a human boy inside. "That's not beef Wellington," you say.

"I know, I know," Fee Fie says. "But I found him sneaking into the castle. And I thought he looked tasty." The boy tries to scramble out, but Fee Fie takes the lid from you and slams it back down on the pot. "I wanted to make a special treat for you," Fee Fie says. "If only I had some beans for my stew."

"I think a bean plant has sprouted up in our garden," you say. "You could go and pick some." After Fee Fie scurries from the kitchen, you open the lid of the pot and scoop out the boy.

"Are you going to eat me?" the boy asks.

"No, no, boys taste terrible," you say. "Like uncooked spaghetti and mushrooms." The boy scrunches up his nose in disgust.

"You'd better get out of here before my wife comes back. She isn't a fussy eater like me. Now get going. I'll just throw in your smelly socks and add some meat from the freezer," you say. "She'll never know the difference."

Without even a word of thanks the boy disappears out of the kitchen. You add the new ingredients to the stew and soon Fee Fie comes back with a handful of beans. You stir the pot, trying to look innocent.

"Oh drat," Fee Fie says, looking into the pot and seeing the sock. "I forgot to undress him before throwing him in."

39

"Adds fibre," you say, kissing her cheek before you leave the kitchen to let her finish cooking.

TO GO FOR A WALK, TURN TO PAGE 40.

TO GO FOR A NAP, TURN TO PAGE 42.

You decide to go for a stroll. You head over to the pond near to where your goose that lays golden eggs lives. As you get close, you hear a loud squawk. Something is wrong! You rush towards the sound. You see the boy – the one you just saved from being stewing meat. He is chasing your goose around the pond.

"Stop that!" you shout. But he doesn't stop. He picks up your goose and makes a run for it. *Why that ungrateful little…*

The boy heads to the beanstalk. With the goose clutched under one arm, he hops down into the chasm. You run for the beanstalk at top speed, but a lumbering giant does not stop quickly. You grab the stalk to slow yourself down, but the beanstalk seems to grab back. It is growing again, sending out shoots that wrap themselves around your ankles.

The beanstalk keeps growing, yanking you off your feet. You are pulled up into the clouds. As your home disappears below, you hope that the stalk isn't taking you to a land where giant giants live.

THE END

TO FOLLOW ANOTHER PATH, **TURN TO PAGE 9.**

Soon your snores are rattling the castle windows. But before long you are woken by loud singing. "Oh mercy me, there is a thief, where's he taking me?"

You blink your eyes open to see the boy you rescued from Fee Fie's pot running past your door. He has your magic harp. The magic harp that sings lullabies to you.

You jump to your feet, toppling stacks of coins across your desk and onto the floor. "Ahhhhh!" you scream. Now you're really angry. You run after the boy and catch him just as he is about to slide into the hole that the beanstalk created. You pick him up by the scruff of his neck as he shouts, "Don't hurt me!"

Luckily for him, you have other plans. "You just wasted a day's worth of my work, lad," you say. "You're coming with me."

You carry the boy to your counting chamber and plop him down onto your desk. "Now count! All of them!" you boom.

The boy begins counting and you put your feet up while he works. You aren't sure yet what you will do with him. You might just keep him to count your coins for you. Or perhaps you'll let Fee Fie finally try that blood of an Englishman recipe she's always talking about.

THE END

TO FOLLOW ANOTHER PATH, TURN TO PAGE 9.

CHAPTER 3

KEEP REACHING FOR THE STARS

You sit at the kitchen table and wait for your son, Jack, to return. You can't start the dinner. You have nothing to cook.

As you tap your fingers impatiently on the table, you wonder why you sent Jack in the first place. After all, he's never been good at following instructions. Earlier today you asked him to go and milk the cow, Milky White. He spent most of the morning walking around the pasture with a bucket over his head pretending to be a robot. Milky was probably too confused or too afraid to produce any milk. And now you're waiting for him to return from trading away poor old Milky White. You just hope he got something more than a handful of beans for her.

45

TURN THE PAGE.

Hours later Jack bursts through the door. He's wearing a big grin, obviously thinking he's done well. He puts a handful of rusty nuts and bolts on the kitchen table. "They're magic!" he says.

Jacks waits for your reply, but his grin slowly fades as he sees your look of disappointment. "We can make something with them," he suggests.

"What, nut and bolt stew?" you yell.

Tears well up in Jack's eyes. Then he rushes up the ladder to his bed in the loft. You feel guilty, but you just couldn't help yourself. You had been hoping for a decent meal tonight, and what did you get? Nuts and bolts.

"Magic?" you mutter. You grab the nuts and bolts, stomp over to the window and fling them out. "That's what I think of magic!"

You feel like banging your head against the kitchen table. At least that would make you forget the hunger pangs wrenching your tummy. But just as you turn away from the window, you hear a clink. Then a clank. Then a colossal clattering begins.

You turn back to the window. To your amazement, sticks, rocks, broken rake handles, chicken wire and just about everything else lying out in the farmyard is whirling about in the air. The objects click together, held in place by the magic nuts and bolts, which seem to be multiplying as quickly as they are needed.

47

Leaning out of the window, you watch a tower of scrap rise up from your yard and shoot skyward. It quickly disappears into the clouds. *What on Earth?* you wonder.

TO CLIMB THE TOWER, TURN TO PAGE 48.

TO TELL JACK ABOUT THE TOWER, TURN TO PAGE 63.

You rush outside, excited. You've never seen such a thing! The tower of scrap twists like a corkscrew, spiralling into the sky. You shake your head in amazement. Magic nuts and bolts! You've got to see where it goes.

As you begin to climb, you can't help but chuckle. You're doing exactly what Jack would do – something foolish and crazy! You have no idea where this tower actually goes or if it's even safe. It creaks and rattles as you climb. But you keep going. You've heard of pots of gold at the end of rainbows. Perhaps this tower will lead to something like that. Or at least to a pot of beef stew.

You move quickly, perhaps even magically. You climb through the clouds, past the moon and into the blackness of space. Up ahead, a red dot grows larger and larger. *Is that Mars?* you wonder.

Your mind spins with the possibilities. Never mind Milky White – you've got access to the whole Milky Way! Even if there isn't any treasure at the end of this tower, you could still charge people for the opportunity to climb it into space. Who wouldn't pay for that chance?

The tower bends down towards the strange planet's rocky red surface. You consider leaping off to go exploring. But just as you're getting ready to jump, you see something in the red sand. It looks like a NASA rover and behind it stands a giant greenish creature with eight limbs and two antennae sprouting from its head. An alien? You've hit the jackpot! You could probably charge a fortune for the chance to meet an extraterrestrial!

49

TO TALK TO THE ALIEN, **TURN TO PAGE 50.**

TO GO AND TELL JACK ABOUT THE ALIEN, **TURN TO PAGE 51.**

You call out to the alien, "Hello! I come in peace." But the alien doesn't hear you. It's banging on the rover with a hammer. You wave your arms wildly and call out again. Finally one of the alien's antennae swivels in your direction. The alien reaches for a gadget hanging from its belt, points it in your direction, and … *ZAP!* Your last thought is, *it serves me right for trying something crazy.*

THE END

TO FOLLOW ANOTHER PATH, TURN TO PAGE 9.

50

You scurry back down the tower. "Jack! Jack!" you shout as you near the ground. He's probably still moping around somewhere. So you call out again. "Jack! Jack!"

Finally he stumbles out of the cottage. "What is it?" he asks, clearly in a bad mood.

"Jack, you were right!" You tell him what happened when you threw the magic nuts and bolts out of the window. And about what you saw after climbing the tower. But he doesn't believe it.

"Mum, are you trying to teach me a lesson? Everybody knows that life doesn't exist on Mars," he says sullenly.

TURN THE PAGE.

You throw up your arms. This from a boy who once claimed he'd been on a giant-slaying adventure? He must still be upset about getting told off earlier.

"Jack, this could be the answer to our prayers!" you say excitedly. "People would pay a fortune to visit Mars and meet a creature from another planet. We could even set up a little gift shop and sell T-shirts and … and…"

"OK, Mum, you can stop. You've made your point. I'll stop believing in magic," Jack says, getting angry. He thinks you're making fun of him. You've got to convince him that, this time, he was right.

52

TO GO BACK TO GET PROOF THAT YOU SAW AN ALIEN,
GO TO PAGE 53.

TO MAKE JACK GO AND SEE FOR HIMSELF, TURN TO PAGE 61.

"Fine," you say. "I will get proof that I saw an alien."

"Could you also bring back a snack?" Jack asks. "I'm starving."

Your blood begins to boil. "You – you," you stammer in anger. He's the one who swapped Milky White for a handful of scrap metal! And he has the nerve to complain about being hungry?

Then Jack says, "So, if what you say is true, and we can make some money, do you think we could get Milky White back? I miss her."

Seeing Jack so sad makes all your anger wash away. You bite your tongue, hoping that Milky White hasn't **53** been made into shoe leather by now. You give Jack a quick hug and climb back up, determined to prove to him that his magic nuts and bolts just might save the family from starvation.

TO STEAL AN ARTEFACT FROM THE ALIEN, **TURN TO PAGE 54.**

TO ASK THE ALIEN TO COME HOME WITH YOU, **TURN TO PAGE 58.**

When you get back to Mars, the alien has pushed the rover into a hole and is busy throwing sand on top of it. You spy what seems to be the alien's bag of supplies near by. Perhaps you can find some proof in there to take back.

You sneak over to it and reach inside. You pull out some sort of crystal with strings attached. A musical instrument? Then, to your surprise, the thing sings out, "Earthlings, Earthlings are invading the stars. They can't know there's life on Mars!"

The alien's antennae whirl around to face you. The alien pulls a gadget from its belt and aims it at you.

You don't wait to find out what the gadget does – you doubt it will be good.

You run, which turns out to be a wise choice, because there's a blinding flash of light and then a smoking black spot in the sand where you were just standing.

You jump onto the tower and start climbing as fast as you can. The alien follows, but luckily it moves as slowly as a snail, and you're able to keep your lead.

When you get within shouting distance of the house, you call out, "Jack! Jack! Grab a spanner!"

Jack comes out of the house just as you reach the ground. For once he has listened and he's carrying a spanner. You take it and start loosening nuts and bolts at the speed of a racing-car mechanic.

"Is that the alien?" Jack asks, looking up the beanstalk. "What's it pointing at us?"

TURN THE PAGE.

"Watch out!" you scream, pushing Jack aside as another flash of light burns a black spot into the ground right next to him.

You loosen the next bolt, and the tower begins to sway and shudder. Then it slowly tips. You jump back, pulling Jack with you.

The tower crumbles, and the alien crashes down with it. When the dust settles, you are left with a mess all over the farmyard, including one dead alien. Before your eyes, the alien melts into the ground, leaving a large green stain. Well, there goes that money-making opportunity, you think.

"What are we going to do now?" Jack cries. "We still don't have a cow or any food, and now we don't even have our magic nuts and bolts."

After selling the alien crystal for a small fortune, you have enough money to buy a lifetime supply of stew ingredients.

You also buy back Milky White, who retires to the pasture to graze out her last days. Finally you buy a young cow, Milky White Too, who likes to play robots as much as Jack does – after she's been milked.

THE END

TO FOLLOW ANOTHER PATH, TURN TO PAGE 9.

This time, when you see the alien, you walk up to it and tap it on the shoulder. "Um, excuse me," you say.

It doesn't turn to look at you, but one antenna twists around and prods at your head.

"Hello! My name's Emma … from Earth. Ah, I have a favour to ask. My son doesn't believe you exist," you say. "If it's not too much trouble, would you mind coming home with me to meet him?"

To your surprise, the alien nods. *You see? It always pays to be polite!* you think. You lead the alien down the tower.

When you are almost home, you are shocked to hear the alien speaking. You thought perhaps he couldn't talk.

"Have-you-told-an-y-one-else-a-bout-me?" it asks in a stilted voice.

"Just my son, Jack," you say.

"That-is-good," it says.

You aren't sure why that is good but don't concern yourself about it. Perhaps the alien isn't very good at small talk. When you get to the bottom of the tower, you bellow, "Jack! I'm back. And look who I brought back with me! Um…" You look at the alien. "I'm sorry. I didn't catch your name."

"Bliztletop," it says.

"Pardon me?" you ask but then say, "Oh, never mind. Jack, I brought back the alien!"

59

A few seconds later, Jack saunters outside. "See," you say, turning to point at the alien. As you do, you realize that the alien is pointing something at you. Something that looks like a weapon.

"Take-me-to-your-lead-er," it says.

TURN THE PAGE.

With a very dangerous looking weapon pointed at you and Jack, what choice do you have?

The alien says, "We-are-tired-of-Earth-lings-send-ing-rov-ers-to-Mars. How-would-you-feel-if-we-treat-ed-your-plan-et-like-a-rubb-ish-dump?" Then it goes on to explain that it's leading an invasion of Earth to teach you a lesson. Soon thousands more aliens are climbing down your tower. Now being poor is the least of your problems.

The next time you have a cow to take to market, you'll just do it yourself.

THE END

TO FOLLOW ANOTHER PATH, TURN TO PAGE 9.

You are annoyed that Jack doesn't believe you, especially after all the odd things he has tried convincing you of in the past. So you tell him – no, order him – to go and see for himself.

"OK. OK, I'll go," he says, looking at you as though you're crazy. He begins his climb and is quickly out of sight.

You wait for him. And wait. You're not sure how long it took you to climb the tower, but the afternoon is quickly turning into night. Part of you worries what Jack will do up on Mars. As you've found out many times before, that boy in unpredictable. And sometimes – usually – his mischief leads to trouble.

61

Suddenly, up in the sky where the tower disappears, you see a flash of light. Then a roaring blast knocks you to the ground.

TURN THE PAGE.

Pieces of the tower come crashing down. You have to roll out of the way to avoid injury. Once the explosion is over, you see that the tower is no longer standing. Even worse, Jack is gone.

"Jack! Oh, why did I send him up there?" you wail. You scramble among the rubble, looking for the magic nuts and bolts, hoping the tower can somehow be rebuilt. But it's no use.

Desperate, you call NASA to ask for their help. After they have finished laughing at your far-fetched story, they say that the next Mars mission isn't for five more years.

"I hope Jack can survive by his wits for that long," you mumble, and then you realize your mistake. *Wits? Who am I kidding? He'll be better off looking for more magic.*

THE END

TO FOLLOW ANOTHER PATH, TURN TO PAGE 9.

"Jack! Jack!" you shout. "Look! Those nuts and bolts. They *were* magic!"

Jack comes out of the house, his eyes puffy from crying. But he's instantly cheered when he sees the tower. "Does it reach all the way to the stars?"

"Who knows?" you say. "But isn't it amazing? We could sell tickets. We could be rich…"

But before you can finish, Jack is scurrying up the tower. "I've got to see this!" he shouts.

"Wait!" you call. Won't that boy ever listen?

63

You want to go up after him to make sure it's safe, but you wonder if you should wait here.

TO WAIT FOR JACK, TURN TO PAGE 64.

TO RUSH UP AFTER JACK, TURN TO PAGE 68.

As you wait, impatiently tapping your foot on the ground, you stare up at the sky. You hope this isn't going to be like the time Jack ran off and almost got boiled up in a giant's pot of stew. At least that's what he said happened…

Suddenly you see a flash high up in the sky. Then a loud *BOOM!* reaches you.

What on Earth was that? you wonder. Then the tower begins to wobble and sway.

TO CLIMB UP TO SEE IF JACK IS OK, **GO TO PAGE 65.**

TO TRY TO STEADY THE TOWER, **TURN TO PAGE 66.**

You have to find out what is happening. As you're climbing, you are surprised at how fast you travel. Soon you are above the clouds and then in the blackness of space.

The tower shudders again, but you keep going. You must get to Jack before anything bad happens to him!

You climb past the moon and then continue on to a reddish planet that you think must be Mars. Once you get close, you see Jack up ahead. He's already on the planet, and he's in trouble. An alien with six arms and antennae is chasing after him. And in one of its many hands it's holding something that looks like a weapon.

65

"Jack!"

TURN TO PAGE 70.

You are afraid to climb up with the tower quivering the way it is, and you are afraid that Jack might fall if it continues to sway. You do everything you can to steady it, roping it to nearby trees and even hugging it with all your might to steady it. But the swaying only gets worse.

Then you see Jack. He's climbing down fast – almost falling. His feet hit the ground just as the tower gives one last shudder, then comes crashing down. You cower under a tree to get out of the way of falling debris.

When the dust settles, you crawl through the wreckage that was once your house. Pieces of the tower lay everywhere.

"Jack!" you screech.

Jack crawls out of the ruins of your house. And he's giggling, which only makes your blood boil. Your house has been destroyed, he could have been killed and he's giggling?

You're about to yell at him when he lifts up a small sack for you to take.

"What's this?" you ask.

"I'm not sure, but they look valuable," he says.

You peer into the sack. It's full of shiny rocks that glint in the sun.

"That's money on Mars," Jack explains. "The alien said I could have it if we promise not to tell anyone there's really life on Mars."

Part of you wonders if Jack is telling stories again, and part of you just doesn't care. Your stomach rumbles and you rattle the sack of pebbles. "Perhaps we can convince someone they're magic and swap them for a cow," you say with a smile.

67

THE END

TO FOLLOW ANOTHER PATH, TURN TO PAGE 9.

You want to make sure that Jack is safe. And, frankly, you want to make sure he doesn't ruin this opportunity – it could make you rich! After all, there could be a pot of gold up there. Or a harp-playing alien, or a flock of magic geese, for heaven's sake! You need to make sure Jack doesn't mess things up.

You start to climb and finally, exhausted, you reach a red planet. All seems quiet. "Jack?" you call, but no one answers. You wander around, calling "Hello? Anybody there?" You begin to have doubts that this boring place could be a money-making opportunity after all. There's nothing here but red sand and rocks.

Then suddenly you hear a strange voice. It keeps repeating the same thing, but you can't quite make it out.

Then it gets louder, and from behind an especially big red rock comes a multiple-headed, many-antennaed creature, lurching towards you like a zombie. Finally you can make out what it's saying: "Fee-fie-fo-fum! I-smell-the-blood-of-an-Earth-ling-man!"

"I'm not a man!" you say, indignant. But that doesn't seem to matter to the creature, which plods towards you. You panic when you find that your feet have sunk into the red sand, and you can't move.

Your money problems no longer matter. It turns out that Earthling women are just as good as Earthling men when it comes to adding flavour to alien stew.

THE END

TO FOLLOW ANOTHER PATH, TURN TO PAGE 9.

Jack ducks behind the tower as the alien fires again. Every time the laser hits the tower, it shudders and pieces of it rain down. If this continues, the tower could collapse.

"Didn't I teach you not to talk to strangers?" you shout as you crawl closer to Jack. And that alien, with its arms and antennae, is about the strangest stranger you've ever seen.

Jack climbs up next to you. "We've got to go!" he shouts. "I took this." He holds up a creature that looks like a cross between a slug and a duck. "I saw it eat a rock, and then, a minute later, a golden nugget came out its other end!"

"You stole it?" you ask.

Jack rolls his eyes. "Mum! We're starving, remember?"

TO FLEE WITH THE SLUG-DUCK, **TURN TO PAGE 72.**

TO GIVE THE SLUG-DUCK BACK, **TURN TO PAGE 74.**

Just then, a laser blast strikes the tower. It groans and creaks. It won't stand much more blasting.

"OK, let's go!" you shout to Jack.

He follows as you slide back down the tower. Above you, you see the alien leap from the planet and grab hold of the tower. Then it also starts to descend.

"We have to hurry!" you shout. "And when we get to the bottom, get the blowtorch."

Once your feet hit the ground, Jack does as you asked – for once! You set to work severing the tower with the blowtorch.

The alien is still descending, but before it gets within shooting range, the tower begins to topple like a giant metal tree.

You and Jack dive into the cellar to take cover.

When all is quiet, you carefully lift the cellar door. The tower has collapsed and formed a cage around the alien.

"What are we going to do now?" Jack asks, hugging the slug-duck tightly. So tightly that a nugget pops out.

"Call NASA. Tell them we'll swap the alien for a good dairy cow."

With Milky White II and a steady supply of gold from your new pet, Sluggie, you and Jack live happily ever after.

73

THE END

TO FOLLOW ANOTHER PATH, TURN TO PAGE 9.

"No wonder the alien is trying to zap you!" you shout. "Here, let me have that." You take the creature from Jack, and then you start waving it in the air.

"Yoo-hoo! Here you go, Mr Alien!" you shout. "You can have your … pet back."

The alien stops firing. It lowers its weapon and simply watches you. So you crawl from your hiding spot. You creep towards the alien, holding out the slug-duck as an offering.

"Here you go," you say. "I'm sorry, but Jack can be a little troublesome. It's just that he's so hungry."

The alien takes the slug-duck from you. "Does-an-y-one-know-you-are-here?" it asks.

"Um, no," you say.

"Good," it says. "Come-with-me."

You'd prefer not to, but then the alien points its weapon at you. You decide you'd better follow. "Where are you taking us?" you ask.

"A-li-ens-will-pay-lots-of-mon-ey-to-see-Earth-lings," it says. You and Jack look at each other quizzically.

The alien leads you to a place that you suppose must be a Martian zoo. There are cages and containers filled with all sorts of odd things. Some look like moving balls of slime. Others have more legs than you can count. It occurs to you that you and Jack may be the oddest things of all here. The alien places you both in an empty cage, and that's where you spend the rest of your days. You're one of the zoo's most popular attractions. But at least you are well fed.

75

THE END

TO FOLLOW ANOTHER PATH, TURN TO PAGE 9.

CHAPTER 4

THE JACKS TEAM UP

Of course, you could have traded old Milky White in for some cash. But what would that have got you — a sack of potatoes and some carrots? Then you'd be eating stew for weeks and, frankly, you don't like stew that much! Especially your mother's.

It's not as though she expected you to make a good deal anyway. Your mother doesn't have much faith in you. She says you're a procrastinator. A rascal. A scallywag. You looked up all those words — they are just different ways of saying you're lazy and naughty.

77

But this time you'll show her! Somehow you're sure what you've got will change your lives – not just provide a few more bowls of stew.

When you get home you throw down the little pieces of metal on the kitchen table and announce, "Magic jacks!" You step back and wait for your mother to tell you what a great son you are.

First she squints her eyes and scrunches up her nose as though she just got a whiff of a smelly shoe. Next the colour of her face changes from a light pink to a violent purple. Then she opens her mouth and screams explode out of her: "JACKS? WHAT WERE YOU THINKING? OLD TOYS?"

She scoops up the jacks and throws them out of the kitchen window. Then she grabs you by the ear and marches you to your room.

With one final shout – "NO DINNER FOR YOU!" – she slams the door.

You shrug. You didn't think there was anything to eat in the house anyway.

In the morning, before your mum wakes up, you sneak out to find the magic jacks. Perhaps you'll be able to swap them for a couple of eggs and a loaf of bread, and surprise her with breakfast. But what you find outside aren't the "jacks" you expected. Instead, you find several boys, all called Jack. They're clustered into two groups – a group of four boys and a group of three.

79

TO GREET THE GROUP OF 4 JACKS, TURN TO PAGE 80.

TO GREET THE GROUP OF 3 JACKS, TURN TO PAGE 98.

"I'm Jack Horner," a boy from the larger group says as you approach. He holds a messy, half-eaten pie out to you. "Plum pie?"

You say no thanks. Then Horner introduces you to three other Jacks. Jack Frost has hair as white as snow. Jack Hill has got a bandage wrapped around his head and mumbles something about his girlfriend, Jill. And Jack Builder says, "I build stuff," pointing to his hammer.

"Why are you here?" you ask the Jacks.

"You summoned us with the magic jacks," Jack Horner explains, licking his thumbs.

"We're here to take you on an adventure," Jack Frost adds, a puff of steam escaping from his lips.

"To battle a giant," Jack Hill whimpers, placing a helmet on his head.

"To steal his treasure," Jack Builder says, swinging his hammer like a club.

"Well, I suppose fighting a giant can't be any worse than facing my mother today" you say.

You've heard rumours about the giant who lives on the mountain. He's a maneater. Or, rather, a boy-eater. You question the wisdom of going to look for him with a group of other boys, but perhaps there will be safety in numbers.

TURN THE PAGE.

The trek to the mountain doesn't take long. The worst part of it all is the Jacks, actually. Jack Hill has fits of sobbing about losing Jill. Jack Horner keeps finding odd nuts and berries he wants to make into pies. The ground around Jack Frost is always icy, causing you to slip and slide. And Jack Builder picks up every stick and stone he finds – to build more houses, he says.

Once you reach the foot of the mountain, you all look up. "I know the quickest way up," Jack Hill offers.

"Are you sure you don't mean the quickest way down?" Jack Frost jokes, referring to Hill's tumble with this Jill person he can't stop talking about. "Let me lead. I know what I'm doing."

TO FOLLOW JACK HILL UP THE MOUNTAIN, GO TO PAGE 83.

TO FOLLOW JACK FROST UP THE MOUNTAIN, TURN TO PAGE 84.

"Jill and I used to climb up this mountain," Jack Hill sobs. You've heard just about enough of his whining. You decide to let him lead. You and the other Jacks follow him from a distance so you won't have to listen to him anymore.

But suddenly you see a boulder crashing down on Jack Hill. *Splat!* Luckily you are far enough back to not get squashed.

"Look!" Jack Horner shouts. "The giant!" Towards the top of the mountain you see a huge figure. He's holding another large rock over his head.

"I know what to do!" Jack Builder yells.

"There's no time for building. I've got a plan!" Jack Frost yells back.

83

TO FOLLOW JACK BUILDER'S PLAN, TURN TO PAGE 85.

TO FOLLOW JACK FROST'S PLAN, TURN TO PAGE 86.

"I know the way up the mountain," Jack Frost says, "because I covered its top in snow." He quickly scampers up as you and the other Jacks follow.

Near the top of the mountain is a cave. You peek inside. Off to one side is a sleeping giant, curled up in a large chair and hugging a golden harp. Around the rest of the cave you see incredible treasures – golden statues, sacks overflowing with gold coins, and even a golden goose locked in a golden cage.

"Who's willing to go in?" you whisper over the giant's snores.

84

"I can sneak in," Jack Hill says. "I once stole a pail of water, and no one even noticed."

"No, let me," Jack Horner says. "I'm a good boy!"

TO SEND JACK HORNER IN, TURN TO PAGE 92.

TO SEND JACK HILL IN, TURN TO PAGE 94.

"Jack Builder, do something!" you cry. You decide the boy with the hammer is your best bet. Jack Builder sets to work gathering twigs and grass. The giant looks down in amusement. In no time Jack has built a large shield that you and the other Jacks hide behind.

"Come on, Jack!" you call to Jack Builder.

"I think I can reinforce it with some vines!" he replies. But by now the giant has lost his patience.

Boom! He throws the first boulder, which rumbles down the hill, barely missing you. *Thud!* The second one gets Horner and Frost. *Crack!* The third boulder comes straight for you, but Jack Builder has pulled out his tape measure. "Jack!" you yell.

85

Splat! The shield that Jack built doesn't protect any of you after all.

THE END

TO FOLLOW ANOTHER PATH, TURN TO PAGE 9.

"Jack Frost, how quickly can you do something?"

Jack Frost inhales deeply and puffs out a breath of icy air. At the giant's feet, a small patch of ice instantly forms. The giant's foot slides sideways, causing him to do the splits and throw the rock straight up into the air. He howls in pain. When the rock crashes down, it lands on the giant with a loud crunch, silencing his howls.

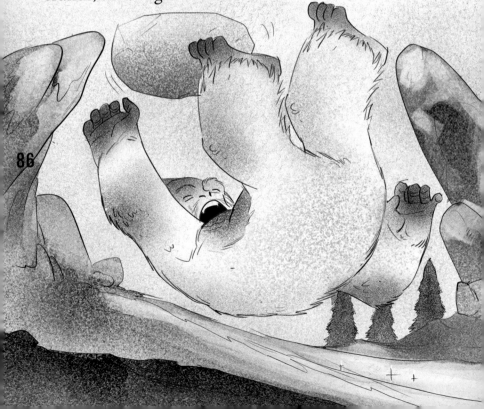

"I think he's unconscious!" Jack Horner says.

"Let's hurry to his cave and get that treasure!" Jack Builder says.

The four of you dash up the hill as fast as you can, careful to skirt around the fallen giant. At the mouth of the cave you stop in amazement as you see the treasures inside. You want to go and get some, but you also want to keep an eye on the giant to make sure he doesn't wake up.

TO GO IN AND GRAB SOME TREASURE, **TURN TO PAGE 88.**

TO ASK JACK HORNER TO GET THE TREASURE, **TURN TO PAGE 92.**

"Wait here, quietly," you whisper to the Jacks. "And keep an eye on that giant!"

Inside the cave you wonder what to take. There are golden goblets, golden statues and even a golden goose in a golden cage. But your eyes land on a golden harp and a large sack of gold coins sitting on a table. The golden harp with its sparkly gems makes you think of your mother. Giving her something so beautiful might get you out of her bad books. Of course with the gold coins you could buy her whatever she wants.

TO CHOOSE THE GOLDEN HARP, GO TO PAGE 89.

TO CHOOSE THE SACK OF GOLD, TURN TO PAGE 91.

You reach up and snatch the golden harp. Immediately it starts to loudly sing, "Put me back, you scoundrel, Jack!" You're wondering what "scoundrel" means when you hear the other Jacks.

"It's the giant!" Jack Frost shouts.

"He's waking up!" Jack Horner adds.

"I could build him a cage," Jack Builder suggests.

You tell the harp, "Shh! I'm going to throw you down the mountain if you wake the giant!"

Suddenly the harp switches to a soft lullaby. "Hush, little baby, don't say a word..." You tiptoe out of the cave with the harp. The other Jacks are nervously watching the giant, who's snoring again.

"It's working," Jack Horner whispers.

"We should leave, now!" Jack Frost says.

TURN THE PAGE.

"I could still build him a cage," Jack Builder suggests.

"I'm getting out of here," you say. Frost and Horner go too. The journey home is less annoying. There's no Jack Hill, sobbing about his girlfriend, and Jack Builder stays behind to build the cage. And Frost and Horner eventually say goodbye as they have other boys to help.

Back at home, you show your mother the magic harp. You expect her to be happy. But, of course, she's not. "Did you steal that, you little thief?" she shouts. You try to explain, but it's no use.

90

"Return it! Now!" she screams. You head back towards the mountain. You hope that the cage Jack Builder made actually works, or you probably won't make it back.

THE END

TO FOLLOW ANOTHER PATH, TURN TO PAGE 9.

You grab the sack of gold and hoist it over your shoulder. Outside the cave Jack Horner tries to help. But when he swings the bag onto his shoulder, he bumps into Jack Frost. Which causes a stream of ice to burst from Frost's fingers onto the ground. Which causes Jack Builder to slide right into the giant.

"Sorry," Frost says sheepishly. "It slipped out."

The giant sits up with a roar. He scoops up Jack Builder and hurls him at you and the other Jacks. You all go flying back into the cave like bowling pins and then you pass out.

When you wake up, you find yourself in a large stewing pot filled with potatoes, turnips and Jacks. "Oh no, I hate stew," you whine as the giant bangs the lid shut.

THE END

TO FOLLOW ANOTHER PATH, TURN TO PAGE 9.

You send Jack Horner to get the treasure while you keep watch – over the giant and the other Jacks.

After a few minutes, you peek inside the cave and see that Horner is staring at a golden cage. Inside is a large golden goose.

"What are you doing?" you whisper, afraid to wake the giant.

Jack Horner ignores you. He reaches into the cage and pulls out a golden egg. "I can make a wonderful pie with this," he says dreamily.

"No!" you hiss. "No pies!"

Just then you hear a scream.

You turn to see the giant launching Jack Builder down the mountain like a human dart. The giant grabs you in his big hairy hand and shoots you through the air. You land with a thud right outside your front door just as your mother is coming out.

"What a layabout," she clucks and steps over your lifeless body.

THE END

TO FOLLOW ANOTHER PATH,
TURN TO PAGE 9.

"OK," you say to Jack Hill. "Go and fetch a sack of gold."

To your surprise, he nimbly darts into the cave and does just as you ask. But he stumbles on his way back, and the sack of gold goes flying through the air. It lands in your arms but several coins fall to the ground with a clatter. The noise causes the giant to stir. One eye opens and focuses on you.

"Let's get out of here!" you shout. With the sack of gold in your arms, you turn and run. Jack Hill is right behind you. And right behind him, you hear the thuds of giant footsteps.

94

Outside the cave you see Jack Frost standing next to an ice slide. Jack Builder stands next to a large wagon he has clearly just constructed. They both wave at you.

TO GO TO JACK FROST, GO TO PAGE 95.

TO GO TO JACK BUILDER, TURN TO PAGE 96.

You and the others jump on Frost's slide and shoot down the mountainside. But the giant does the same. At the bottom he slams into all of you, scattering Jacks everywhere. You groan in pain and think there's no escaping now. But instead of hearing an angry roar, you hear a roar of laughter.

"Fee-Fie-Fo-Fum. That's the most fun thing I've ever done!" Then the giant slings all of you over his shoulder and heads back up to do it again.

"I won't survive another go!" Jack Hill sobs, rubbing his head.

"You should have used my wagon," Jack Builder complains, clutching his back.

"You'll slide and you'll like it!" you order the boys, while pocketing a few stray pieces of gold.

THE END

TO FOLLOW ANOTHER PATH, TURN TO PAGE 9.

You notice the racing stripes that Jack Builder has somehow had time to paint and decide the wagon looks like too much fun to pass up. You and the Jacks jump in. The wagon starts rolling, building speed quickly. The good thing is you zoom away from the giant. The bad thing is..."Where are the brakes?" Jack Hill sobs.

"I didn't have time to build them," Builder admits.

"But you had time for racing stripes?" you bellow.

"AHH!" everyone screams as you bounce through trees and rocks. A big bump launches Jack Hill out of the wagon. Another bump and Jack Frost flies into the air. The next bump sends Jack Builder into the uppermost branches of a tree.

You are the last one in the wagon as it crashes into the side of your house, gold coins from your bag raining down on you. As you lay on the ground groaning in pain, your mother steps outside.

"Why, Jack!" she shouts with glee. "It looks like those jacks were magic after all. It's raining gold coins! Good boy!" Then she points to the broken pieces of wagon and growls, "Now stop lying around and clean up this mess!"

97

Despite your bumps and bruises, you smile to yourself, glowing from your mother's praise.

THE END

TO FOLLOW ANOTHER PATH. **TURN TO PAGE 9.**

"Jack Sprat's the name," a skinny boy from the smaller group says. He's holding an empty plate, which he is licking clean. Next he introduces you to Lazy Jack, who's leaning against a colourful box, dozing, and finally to Jack Box.

"Who?" you ask, looking around.

"Hello there!" a muffled voice shouts from within the box.

"Oh, so you're Jack *in the* Box," you clarify. "What are you all doing here?" you ask.

"We're the magic jacks," Jack Sprat explains, giving the plate a last lick. "We're here to help you."

"To prove to your mother that you're not a good-for-nothing," Jack Box's muffled voice adds from inside.

Sprat nudges Lazy Jack. "Huh? Oh, so, how can we help?" Lazy Jack asks with a yawn.

You look at the tall mountain poking into the clouds. You've heard a giant lives there and that he has unimaginable treasures. "There!" you shout, pointing to the mountain. "I want to find the giant, steal his treasure and give it to my mother."

"Then we shall call you Jack the Giant Slayer!" Sprat claps in excitement.

You didn't mention anything about slaying, but you don't correct him. "How shall we get there?" you ask.

Jack Box says he has a plan, but through the box it sounds like, "Uh haff a ham." Suddenly Lazy Jack snorts awake again and chimes in, "I know a short cut."

TO LISTEN TO JACK BOX'S PLAN, TURN TO PAGE 100.

TO USE LAZY JACK'S SHORT CUT, TURN TO PAGE 104.

"Climb on to the lid of my box," Jack Box offers. You and Jack Sprat hop up and drag Lazy Jack along. A tune starts playing. Then the music stops and the lid springs open. You and the others rocket through the air and land in a heap on the mountain. "You're welcome!" Jack Box calls from far below.

In front of you is a cave. The giant's cave? One of you needs to investigate.

TO GO INTO THE CAVE, **GO TO PAGE 101.**

TO SEND JACK SPRAT INTO THE CAVE, **TURN TO PAGE 105.**

You decide you'd better be brave and do it. It's your mission after all. Peeking inside, you see a giant sleeping on a golden bed. Around him are countless treasures. Your eyes light up.

"Wait here," you tell the Jacks.

Quietly you creep into the cave. Sacks of gold are piled up along one wall. Golden plates and goblets line shelves, and golden jewellery hangs like stalactites from the roof of the cave. There's even a golden goose in a golden cage. On top of a table, a golden harp catches your eye.

TO TAKE THE GOLDEN HARP, **TURN TO PAGE 102.**

TO TAKE THE GOLDEN GOOSE, **TURN TO PAGE 103.**

You creep over to snatch the harp. But as soon as you grab it, the harp begins to sing, "Help! Attack! Save me from Jack!" You drop the harp, stumble back, and bump into something large. You turn to see the giant towering over you. Under one arm, he's holding the other Jacks.

"You woke me up," he growls. "Now sing me a lullaby so I can get back to sleep." He lays back down and snuggles up with the Jacks as if they're teddy bears. They look at you with pleading eyes.

You begin to sing, "Rock-a-bye baby…" The giant slowly closes his eyes and begins to snore. Still singing, you tiptoe out of the cave. The Jacks glare at you as you escape with the harp. You feel guilty but decide it's every Jack for himself.

THE END

TO FOLLOW ANOTHER PATH, TURN TO PAGE 9.

You've heard about this goose. It lays golden eggs! You and the Jacks scamper home with your prize. "Now your mother won't think you're a good-for-nothing!" Jack Sprat says. You thank the Jacks, say goodbye, then go and show your mother.

"I suppose you brought home a magic goose this time," she sneers.

"And it lays golden eggs!" you say. As if on cue, an egg plops onto the table. Your mother picks it up and taps it on the frying pan. Nothing happens.

"How am I supposed to cook with this?" she asks. She shakes her head in disgust and grabs a knife. "Cooked goose will have to do for breakfast."

103

"No!" you cry, but it's too late. At least roast goose is better than stew.

THE END

TO FOLLOW ANOTHER PATH, TURN TO PAGE 9.

"Lead the way, Lazy Jack," you say.

You follow him around a couple of rocks where a cable car awaits. It takes you up the mountain at what seems a magical speed. Soon you're at the top of the mountain standing in front of the giant's cave.

You look back down the mountain and marvel at Lazy Jack's short cut. "Wow, that really was quick," you say.

"Told you." Lazy Jack sits down and leans against a rock. "But it was still a lot of work," he says. "I'm going to have a nap."

Jack Sprat approaches the mouth of the cave.

Sprat goes inside and a long time passes. You start to feel anxious and nudge Lazy Jack.

"Go and see what happened to Sprat," you say. He disappears and doesn't return either. You suppose it's your turn. You step inside and a meaty fist snatches you up. The giant pokes at you with his beefy finger as he hangs you upside down. "Hmm," he says. "That first one was a bit scrawny, the second one a bit squishy, but you look just about right. Be ye alive or be ye dead, I'll grind your bones to make my bread."

As you look wildly around you see the other Jacks sitting in a pot of water, waving at you sheepishly. It looks like the giant will be having Jack bread with Jack stew tonight.

THE END

TO FOLLOW ANOTHER PATH, TURN TO PAGE 9.

THE MANY JACKS

No one is sure when the story of Jack and the Beanstalk was first told. It's a tale that has been around for hundreds of years. But a version similar to the ones we are familiar with today was first published in the early 1800s. Benjamin Tabart retold the events of Jack and the giant in *The History of Jack and the Bean-Stalk* (1807).

Tabart's retelling starts off the same way as most versions. Jack and his mother are poor. They are forced to sell their cow. On the way into town, Jack meets a man who offers him some magic beans in exchange for the cow. And, of course, Jack accepts the offer.

Tabart gives Jack an excuse, however, for doing the things that he does. In *The History of Jack and the Bean-Stalk*, Jack meets a fairy after climbing up the beanstalk. She tells him that his father was "as rich as a prince". But when Jack was just months old, the giant killed his father and stole all of his father's wealth.

In his retelling, Tabart implies that it is acceptable for Jack to steal from the giant. Jack is only retrieving treasures that should have belonged to him anyway. And by killing the giant in the end, Jack is getting revenge for his father's death.

Joseph Jacobs did not include the fairy in his version of *Jack and the Beanstalk* in 1860. He did not want to promote theft and murder in a story meant for children. So he turned Jack into a mischievous lad. Jack does the things he does, not for revenge, but because he's curious and badly-behaved.

In Tabart's version Jack appears heroic. In Jacobs', he's almost unlikable. One reason for the different versions of Jack is that stories were once told orally. One generation would tell the story to the next generation, and so on. People would remember the story differently over the years, and then retell it the way they remembered it. Jacobs claimed that there wasn't a fairy in the version of *Jack and the Beanstalk* he heard in his youth.

Another reason for different versions is that people's beliefs change over time. As society's views on what's right and wrong change, storytellers adapt stories to fit their values. That is why Jack can be a hero in one version, a villain in another or a lazy youth in yet another.

These variations continue today, from books and films to comics and cartoons. Sometimes Jack meets the fairy and sometimes he does not. Sometimes the giant has a goose that lays golden eggs or a magical talking harp.

Traditional tales will continue to change and evolve as long as writers can think of creative new ways to retell them. And as long as children hear them, remember them, and retell them in their own way to future generations, the stories will live on.